Share the Experience of Reading...

Help a child to confidently and successfully develop a lifelong love of reading.

At Flyleaf Publishing, our mission is to create books for children that:

- **Support reading skill development**
- **Convey the value of reading as a means of communicating ideas**
- **Foster an enjoyment of books that will grow into a lifelong love of reading.**

The Sunset Pond, the first book in the Flyleaf *Books to Remember* collection, combines the beauty of a fine art picture book with a simply written phonetically based text.

- **Phonetic text allows young readers to successfully "sound out" words**
- **Supplementary Learning Cards included in the flyleaf of each book extend the reading experience and increase confidence and comprehension**
- **Fine art illustrations enrich and support the text of the story**

Laura Appleton Smith's carefully written text and Jonathan Bumas' beautiful watercolor and pastel illustrations bring *The Sunset Pond* to life. This is a story full of rich images and childhood fun, making it truly a *Book to Remember.*

Picture Cards

The **Picture Cards and Labels** represent the nouns that your child will encounter in his or her *Flyleaf Book To Remember*. Separate the cards and the labels at their perforated edges. Place the picture cards in one pile, the labels in another. Find a quiet uncluttered location to look through just the picture cards with your child. Discuss the names of the objects on the cards. If there are any names your child does not know, teach them to him or her. Next, lie the picture cards out in an orderly manner, leaving enough space below each card for its label. One at a time, read the label with your child, showing him or her how to say the sound of each letter until the word is recognized. Once the child reads the word, invite him or her to place the label under the matching picture.

Hints: Give assistance when necessary, saying the sound of each letter and "slurring" them together to help your child to hear the word made up by the sounds. Keep the cards in a place where your child can find them and read independently as he or she chooses.

Puzzle Cards

Puzzle Cards represent the sight words or words with phonograms that a child will encounter in this *Flyleaf Book To Remember*. These are words that do not sound the way they look. Separate the cards at their perforated edges. Read through them with your child, then teach them a few at a time like flashcards until your child recognizes them all. Be creative and have fun!

Game Ideas:

1. Place words that your child knows face down on a table. Invite your child to turn them over one at a time and read them.

2. Place the puzzle words that your child knows on a table across the room. Think of a word card and invite your child to bring it to you. Children will love the movement in this game. When they return, ask "What did you bring me?" Invite your child to read the card back to you.

Hints: Be gentle in the correction of errors. Repetition is the key to success in these games. Keeping the reading you do together positive and fun will help your child to enjoy the reading process.

Action Cards

The red **Action Cards** represent the verbs that your child will encounter in this *Flyleaf Book to Remember*. Separate the cards at their perforated edges and place them in a pile. Read through the cards one at a time with your child. If your child does not recognize the word, encourage him or her to say the sounds of the letters until the word is formed.

Ideas: Invite your child to read a verb card and then act out the action. Your child will enjoy watching you be an actor too! Our verb cards are ideal for a simple family game of charades.

The Sunset Pond

Written by Laura Appleton Smith

Illustrated by Jonathan Bumas

Laura Appleton Smith

The paintings in this book were done in transparent and opaque watercolors and pastels.
The text and titling were set in Stone Informal.
This book was printed with 22 percent soy-based inks on Mountie Matte Recycled paper.
Color separations were made by Fox Press Incorporated, Windsor, Connecticut.
Design and production by Kolk Design, Newington, Connecticut.
This book was printed and bound in the United States of America.

A Book to Remember™
Published by Flyleaf Publishing
Post Office Box 185
Lyme, NH 03768

For questions, comments, or orders contact our customer service department at (800) 449-7006.
Please visit our website at www.flyleafpublishing.com

First Edition
Library of Congress Catalog Card Number: 97-61171
ISBN 0-9658246-3-2

Many thanks to the children in my classroom who have helped me to understand the deep value of the early reading experience.

And to Terry–without your support, this book would not be.

LAS

—

For Martha.

JB

It is half past six and the sun has just begun to set in the west. Matt asks his mom and dad if he may run with Bud to the Sunset Pond. Mom and Dad tell Matt, "Yes, but plan to be back at dusk."

Matt and Bud jump from the front steps onto the soft grass. They run past the beds of daffodils and down the hill to the sunset pond.

Matt picks up a stick and tosses it in the pond for Bud.

"Jump in, Bud," yells Matt.

Bud jumps in the pond and swims fast to get the stick.

He huffs and puffs as he grasps it and swims back to Matt.

Bud drops the stick in front of Matt. Matt pats him and tells him that he is the best dog. Bud wags big wet drips on Matt's legs and hands.

Just then Bud stops and scans the pond.

"What is it, Bud?" asks Matt.

In the pond is a log and on the log is a big bull frog.

Bud jumps back in the pond and swims to the frog

as fast as he can.

"Jump, frog, jump!" yells Matt.

Bud swims fast, but just as he gets to the log the frog

hops off and lands with a "plop" in the pond.

The frog is quick to swim into a clump of grass on the bank of the pond. In the grass, the frog is hidden and Bud cannot spot him.

Bud swims back and sits next to Matt on the dock.

Bud naps as Matt skips rocks on the pond.

As the sun slips past the hills in the west, the pond glints red and pink. A duck lands on the pond and drifts in the sunset.

The pond is still.

When it is dusk, Mom claps her hands and Matt and Bud run back up the hill. Matt stops and picks a daffodil for Mom. For Matt and Bud, the pond is the best spot to visit at sunset.

he	to	onto
they	be	with
down	that	may
when	is	half
what	for	the
run	jump	toss
swim	wag	ask
stop	hop	sit
skip	clap	scan
yell	pick	drop